13 FOREVERS

13 FOREVERS

*Stories and
Reflections on
Death and Love*

KEVIN CHABA

For Mia

Forever

TABLE OF CONTENTS

13 FOREVERS

INTRODUCTION

◆ ◆ ◆

It's important to note that, though some of these pieces certainly appear otherwise, everything in this collection was written before my wife died. In fact, they were all written before we even had an inkling that she was sick, except for two ("Eye of the Beholder" and "Not Dying"). Those were written while she was sick but before we knew the prognosis. You don't have to worry; these won't be the maudlin moanings of a widower. These are just some things I wrote to try and impress her. However, they might make *you* feel a little icky and gross inside. They're partly about death, after all.

If she'd never died, I'd never have had any motivation to publish; only her eyes would ever have seen them. I hope that even if they do make you feel gross and icky, there's enough of the "love" side that you can see why she enjoyed them. That way, in some pretending-there's-an-afterlife kind of fashion, a part of my wife will live on—not exactly forever, but close enough for me. I don't believe in an afterlife, but if you enjoy what she enjoyed, then pretending there is one will be enough for me. And anyway, the fact that this work can be found online is pretty great in itself, isn't it? The Internet is probably the closest we humans have gotten so far to something truly eternal—besides, of course, death. And love.

Kevin Chaba
May 2017

1

Love Afterlife

Two corpses rotted side by side for eternity, letting their thoughts wander. For decades, they didn't even know they were neighbors, until sizable adjacent holes had worn away in each of their caskets. Lefty floundered in ennui. Righty's mind flitted anxiously.

Lefty gave names to the worms and beetles. In time, though, all of the normal names had been assigned, so rather grandiose names needed inventing—names like Percivaxlia and Supprinkstein. For a brief, joyful spell, a skunk raised a litter of kits in a burrow that bottomed out into Lefty's domain. Lefty watched the babes like a shepherd dog whenever the mother left. Once, only three of the four kits came back from outside. Lefty was broken-hearted and never forgot the missing youngster's name: Aloysionides.

After the skunks abandoned the hole, a cottonmouth took residence in it for a span made all the more awkward by the snake's messy habits. Lefty didn't bother to name it. Eventually, the den caved in, Lefty's last connection to the living surface.

Righty visualized running, swimming, and driving fast. Arm flesh, now decayed, conferred falcon-feathered flight in Righty's imagination, gazing out, down. Sometimes those particular daydreams brought joy, sometimes irritation.

Life stymied Righty's death. Memories raced fitfully and still panged fresh. In life, someone had cut scars in Righty, the kind that only love can leave. Other lovers had gilded Righty with guilt. Righty had died a rough-shuffled deck of cards, always bound by rubber bands, never put back neatly in a box.

Peace or pieces, it was rest.

When they weren't being bored, Lefty and Righty's thoughts occasionally lighted on each other.

Lefty would've loved to stargaze with Righty and mused about it often. Something about the everythingness made Lefty want to share meditative breaths. As a matter of course, Righty looked up to Lefty.

On the surface, time weathered through seasons. Rock embraced them with the eons, pushing the living soil and bugs and critters up and away. Doleful at their absence, Lefty, skeletal, settled into depression. Righty half-heartedly noticed.

Righty desperately wanted to say something— the caskets had long dissolved between them—

but it just never felt like the right time. Summers and winters blurred innumerably, as harrowingly slow tears formed crystals.

Under just one warm breeze, on just one cloud-and-sun afternoon, in just one October, in just one infinitely small second, Lefty caught Righty's gaze, or maybe Righty caught Lefty's. In the constant changing of their deaths, time went still.

On Righty's wings, together, their thoughts surged away into Lefty's stars!

And, if you and I could see—impossibly—through time to where it ends, through layers of sediment and soil and bugs and grass, through families and names and gravestones, through ourselves like bullet holes, we would smile together upon this: our singular pair, bone now stone, holding hands now ever.

2

The Position

"**R**IDE ME HOME TO HELL, YOU RESPLEN-
DENT STALLION!" They climaxed in per-
fect harmony, then collapsed on the succulently
sticky sheets.

Jane and Mark woke up the next morning
with hangovers of the same magnitude as the
orgasms they'd had the previous night. They
hadn't been that drunk since before the baby,
probably not since college. Jane's stomach com-
manded her to run for the bathroom and Mark
discovered he'd wet the bed. Over strong, black
coffee, they could only discuss one thing.

"That position last night was UHMAZING!"

"It was incredible!" Mark smiled, sore but smug.

"I've never come so hard in my fucking life,
Mark. That position...well, I didn't know there
was a button that could do *that*, but you found it!
You found it sooooo good! We shouldn't've got-
ten so drunk, though. Something could've hap-
pened to Pinky and we would've snored right
through her crying."

"God, I am not looking forward to work today," Mark gingerly massaged the bridge of his nose. "I should head out. I— I love you sweetiecake." Jane beamed up at Mark through misty, dark-ringed eyes.

"I love you too, honeybear."

The pet names, rarely used of late, were a throwback to the passion from when their relationship was new.

◆

At around 4:30 that afternoon, Mark had a thought, and sent Jane a text message. His question embarrassed her a little, because she had to admit she couldn't answer. She decided to wait until Mark got home and feign a missed message.

"Sweetiecake, I'm home!" Mark called out, as he kicked off his shoes. He went straight upstairs to the nursery, where Jane was changing Pinky's diaper.

"Hey, honeybear, welcome home. I missed you today."

Mark's chest swelled. "I missed you too." He gave her a peck on the back of the neck. "Hey, you never answered my text message from, like, forty-five minutes ago."

"What? I guess I didn't see it. What happened?"

"Nothing, it's just…I was trying to think. Do you remember exactly what position we were in last night?"

"You mean *you* don't remember?" She teased.

"We were drunk as hell. I think I was on top?"

"Well, now that you mention it, I guess it's pretty hazy for me, too. I'm ashamed I drank so much."

Intermittently throughout the evening, one or the other of them would try to recall the magical position they'd happened into the previous night. By the time they put Pinky down for the evening, all they could do was fall into bed and sleep.

◆

"Look around online while you're at work, OK?" Jane said. A week had passed since their entrancing tryst. "I'm going to do the same."

"Are you sure? There will be a lot of…junk to wade through. I know how you feel about porn—"

"I'm not looking forward to it. But I'd really like to find that position again."

◆

Nine hours later, neither was any closer to solving the mystery.

"I don't understand. I watched an entire video kama sutra and I didn't find it!" Jane looked up from the computer and rubbed her eyes.

"I tried poking around on Urban Dictionary," Mark said, "but all that really did was give me some funny stuff to email to Carl."

"Oh, goody. Well, at least you tried. A for effort, dummy."

"Hey! That's uncalled for!"

"I saw soooo many penises today, Mark. So many strange, asymmetrical penises."

Mark cocked his head with an idea. "How about the next time we have sex we just, you know, wing it; try and find the position as we go. Worst case, we still get to have sex."

"I suppose."

"Don't sound so sad."

"It was *really* good the other night."

"Yeah it was...." Mark reveled in the memory.

"And I want that again! A new standard has been set!" Jane brandished a letter opener playfully at her husband.

◆

Between Pinky, work, and other stresses, it would be more than a month before Jane and Mark had the energy and opportunity to give it another go.

"Can you...swing your— over here—"

"Maybe if you just—"

"No, I mean your leg—"

"That's *your* leg!"

"Gentle!"

"You're on my hair!"

"What? How is that possible?!"

"I mean my pubic hair!"

"Oop! Sorry."

"I can't balance like this forever!"

"Aahh! Rugburns!"

After a while, they simultaneously threw in the towel and retreated back to their own corners of the mattress. Both of them were panting, a little sore, and feeling defeated.

Over the next six months, every time Mark and Jane tried to get marital, it was the same thing: frustrated maneuvering, resituating, and rethinking the angles until they both surrendered. Pinky moved from a crib to a toddler bed and they still couldn't find the enchanting position in their king-size.

◆

Mark hurried home from work one day, buoyant, to find Jane reading the paper.

"Mark, did you see that iPhones are gonna start having model years, like cars?"

"That's great sweetie, but listen. I think I have a solution to our position problem!" At that, she stood straight up so fast that the *Times* and a teacup spilled onto the floor.

"What?!"

"Come here and pull up another chair to the computer."

When she was settled, he opened the web browser and typed in an address. "This is CopulationElation.org.asm, the biggest sexual discussion forum on the net. Today, I stole a few minutes at work, made an account, and put out a call for help. Millions of people across the world use this site. Given those odds, somebody's bound to send us a link to a video of 'our' position...probably starring a midget and an amputee!"

"I guess it's worth a try. What did you say?"

He pointed to the screen.

URGENT HELP NEEDED!!

Please help save my marriage! My wife and I had the best sex of our lives recently. The problem is that we were so drunk we can't remember the position we were in—and the position was key! All we can remember is that I was on top, and she could look up at me, on the bed. From there, we've been using the process of elimination. It is **NOT** any of the following positions:

Missionary

Leg glider

London bridges

Doggy

Poodle

Screwdriver

Pile Driver

Gomer Pyle driver

Prison guard

Buckingham palace guard

Cowboy

Upside-down transverse cowgirl

Drill baby drill

V for victory

Vatican oyster

Sitting bull

Superdog

Scoliosis

Regular

Please help! What could it possibly be?!

"What do you think, sweetie?"

"I think I need to edit this with all the kama sutra positions I've already rejected. Can we do that?"

Mark figured out how to edit his post and Jane spent the rest of the evening revising it.

They went to bed hopeful for the first time in months.

♦

"THIS IS INSANE!" Jane yelled. "Look at this bull-shit!"

Mark strode into the room. "Jane, sweetie, please try to keep the swearing down. Pinky's really starting to pick up on things."

"Look! All these responses, but none of them are helping! Everyone is suggesting positions we already listed or that don't fit the criteria, or they're just asking us, 'What are you into?' They're morons!" Her voice cracked and she started sobbing.

"Oh, hey! There, there sweetie. Don't give up! It's only been a few days!"

"No....We're never gonna find it and I'll never feel like that again!"

Mark did his best to console his desperate wife and after a while, she agreed to give the web forum more time.

♦

Two years went by.

Jane came home from picking Pinky up at kindergarten to find a plain brown package on the doorstep addressed to her husband. She left it on his chair in the living room without much thought.

When he got home, she pointed at it and said, "Oh, Mark...something came for you today."

"Oh, yeah! Actually, it came for us, if you get my drift."

"What is it?"

"I'll tell you after Pinky goes to bed," he whispered with a wink.

"What happens after I go to bed, Daddy?" said Pinky, waddling over and reaching her arms up toward him.

He picked her up with a grin. "Nothing Pinkysprout. Just boring grownup stuff."

◆

As the night wore on, Jane couldn't sit still.

"But Mommy, how come I have to brush my teeth and take a bath already?"

"You have to go to bed a little early tonight, Pinky. Tomorrow's a big day!"

"Show & Tell's not a big day. We have it every week. I'm gonna bring *The Little Engine That C—*"

"That's nice, Pinkysprout—now scrub-a-dub so we can dry you off."

"But I can't sleep when the sun's still up."

"*Enough!* You're going to bed early tonight because Mommy said so! And if you say one more word about it, so help me, Mommy will *lose her freaking mind!*"

◆

With Pinky finally settled in, Jane strolled into the living room in a see-through teddy, batting her eyelashes.

"What did you have to show me?" She lilted.

Mark just smiled mischievously and said, "Let's go to bed...but not to sleep!"

She giggled and followed him, hope reborn for the first time in months. As she pulled the blankets back, he produced a curvy, purple device that could've passed for a model alien spacecraft.

"This, my lady," Mark announced, "is the answer to our problems. It's the Wimbo brand Cloud 10 G-Joy DLX Edition Intimate Massage System. This vibrator is the cutting edge of female pleasure. It was recommended to me by a sex doctor I found on Angie's List. It was also recommended by his nurse practitioner, his receptionist, and another patient who overheard from the next exam room. It has vibration modes for up-and-down, back-and-forth, cross-hatch, and convex-concave. There are fifty-three vibration patterns and twenty-one speed settings. It connects via Bluetooth to this phone app, which measures orgasm intensity, total orgasms per session and lifetime, and displays a countdown to the next one. It even has verbal commands for me, you know, where and how to hold it based on the configuration of your—" he waved a hand diplomatically—"interior, which it can map in real-time using Echo-Orientation Sonitechnology. It has a rating on Amazon of 34,703 five-stars, and one four-star rating. The four was from a lady who thought she was buying a carpenter's studfinder but decided to keep it anyway. The home website for this bad boy has links to third-party scientific studies that have found quantifiable medical applications for it. There are also testimonials from Kim Kardashian, Former First Lady Laura Bush, and Bruce Willis. This is, by all accounts, the best female sex toy in existence today."

Before he was halfway through his preamble, Jane was spread-eagled on the bed, desperate drool dripping unhindered down her cheek. Mark plugged it in and pulled the ripcord.

◆

Mark and Jane were flipping through the mail over weak decaf one evening, when Mark said,

"What are we going to do? Pinky's college fund is gone, the 401(k) is decimated, and these minimum payments are insane! Visa's gonna turn us over to Collections!"

"We should sell Pinky," Jane said flatly.

"Don't even joke like that."

"I know, I know. But Mark, she started fifth grade last month. Fifth grade! I haven't had a single good—ugh, I can't even say the word—since back when we were measuring her age in months! I don't know how much more I can take, I—"

"It's these useless sex toys! You can't ever return them—and none of them do a goddamn thing!"

After the Wimbo brand Cloud 10 G-Joy DLX Edition Intimate Massage System had failed her, Jane had become obsessed. She'd ordered hundreds of devices that promised the thunder, the lightning, and the pouring rain, but nothing came close to the wonderstorm she'd felt during that one extraordinary night of pleasure. Some had cost more than $1,000, yet each had been used only once before being relegated to a closet.

"Where are we gonna find $4,700 to pay this Mastercard bill?" Mark fretted. The hair at his temples had begun to turn grey.

"The Visa's got twelve," Jane added.

◆

Around the time Pinky started her sophomore year of high school, Mark started cheating. As Jane withdrew further into malaise, her desire for sex with him had all but dried to a husk, and the few semi-spiteful handjobs he wheedled out of her made a pitiful mockery of their former fuck life. He'd earnestly tried to keep her as happy as he could, and often suggested going down on her or using his fingers. She'd experienced only frustration and the mildest, vanilla-flavored orgasms as a result of his efforts.

When Mark's firm hired a new payroll consultant in a pleated miniskirt, he barely even tried to restrain himself from her advances.

Exhaustion, or maybe remorse, kept him careless. Jane found out within weeks. She discovered hotel receipts and noted strange perfume emanating from his work shirts. One night she followed his car and glimpsed him kissing someone in the doorway of a motel before entering without so much as a glance over his shoulder. Jane sobbed and shook the whole drive home. By the time she'd parked the car, she'd decided against confronting Mark. It didn't really surprise her when she thought about it. She'd probably have cheated a decade ago if she'd met anyone she thought could deliver anything akin to that mythic orgasm.

She went inside and tried to masturbate. This time, she couldn't climax whatsoever. Alarms panicked in and out of her heart. Even in the worst of times, she could feel a little something. But now, nothing! She tore apart her collection of toys and devices, which had been relocated to the storage cubby of the small rental apartment they'd been foreclosed into. Furiously, she tried everything, mortally desperate for release that would not come.

Mark came home to find her bawling in the bathtub, fully clothed, with the shower running. "Hey, umm...sweetie....listen, I know this is frustrating...I wish there was something I could do. If you can think of anything that might give you...*real*...pleasure again, I'll try it. Hell, I'll do anything to have sex with you again. I— I love you, sweeticake."

"Let's get drunk."

"What?"

"Let's go off someplace by ourselves and just get completely hammered, like we were that night, when Pinky was a baby. Just drunk, and horny, and pray everything lines up."

◆

Mark made reservations at a bed-and-break-fast along a lake popular with postcard pho-tographers. Pinky was now too old for a sitter, so he arranged for her to stay with a friend. He bought a thirty-pack of Guinness, Bacardi 151, and several wines from France, Spain, and Western New York. From room service, he or-dered candied dates, chocolate-covered straw-berries, and what they called Spanish Fly Souf-flé. He even rented a few pornos he hoped they'd both like.

Some time into their momentous evening, they blacked out.

As they ambled the car home the next morning, enduring hangovers that felt familiar, Mark said, "So...do you remember anything from last night?"

"I remember doing a third shot of 151 and then it gets fuzzy."

"I don't remember anything at all."

"I don't think we had sex."

"Neither do I."

After that, the drive became profoundly qui-et. Jane stared out the window, eyes unfocused. Mark cried without making a sound.

◆

Mark ducked his head into his daughter's bedroom. She already had a banner hanging above her bed from the state college she would be attending in the fall. An aunt had agreed to cosign the loan paperwork, as her parents' credit was in shambles.

"Pink?" She looked up from her iPhone 2029.

"Yeah, dad?"

"Have you seen Mom?"

"Nope...last time I saw her was before school this morning."

"Well, her planner is by the computer and today it just says 'groceries.' She hasn't responded to any of my texts."

Pinky just shrugged.

Day turned to night with no sign of Jane, and Mark stayed up, pacing the few rooms of their flat. At three in the morning, he called the police to report her missing.

◆

Pinky got a degree in Veterinary Science and opened a practice in the same town where she'd attended college. At a prudent age, she and her lover adopted a little boy named Kalil.

Every summer, she returned alone to her

hometown for a somber family visit. Kalil began to ask questions, so one year, she relented and brought him along on the annual pilgrimage. Her better half elected to stay home.

"Here he is, Kalil. Mark Leslie Loisel. Your grandfather. My father."

"What should I do, Momma?"

"Just lay the flowers down in front of the headstone."

"How come he killed himself?"

"I'll explain it all when you're older."

"You say that every year, Momma. I'm eleven now. How come you brought me along if I'm still too young?"

"God, it's been so many years. Are you sure you're ready? Because it isn't...normal."

The boy nodded and Pinky began to speak. As the story unfolded, her son's eyes widened.

They left the cemetery, and she drove them see her mother. Pinky turned in off the county road, past a razor-wire fence, to visitor parking. As they walked through the door of a concrete building, Kalil looked up at a sign reading:

Wedrich R. Durson Hospital
for the Criminally Insane

◆

Five minutes after calling to report her missing, police were knocking on Mark's door. He complimented their expedience profusely, which confused the plainclothes detectives who'd arrived.

"But aren't you here to find my missing wife?"

"We *are* here looking for your wife, Mr. Loisel," explained one surly, tired badge named Driscoll. "But we weren't aware she was reported missing until just now. She's a suspect in—" seeing how close Mark already was to tears, the investigator sighed. "You should probably sit down for this, sir."

Quickly, Mark was crying again, this time in horror instead of worry. He complied with the detectives' requests and accessed Jane's email.

"There's a new one!" Driscoll shouted. "She's meeting someone right now, the address is here! It's close by, let's go!" Mark watched, dumbstruck, as the detectives flew out the door, their siren blaring out a moment later. He looked at the computer screen and a slew of emails filled the inbox. One sender kept coming up, among many he didn't recognize: Craigslist. He found the backlink and what he saw made his heart shatter into shards.

FREE SEX FOR ORGASMS!!!
This is not a joke or a scam. I need it. Bad.

She concluded the post with her email address, and included a picture of herself in a fake diamond necklace and a bra-and-panty set Mark had bought her for some frustrating Valentine's Day half a decade ago.

According to the newest email, Mark realized, Jane was just around the corner. He tore outside, ran past his car, around and up the block. Lungs aching, he approached the crime scene in time to see his wife being led to a police car in shackles, covered in blood. A uniformed officer held Mark from approaching, as Jane screamed into the early morning "I CAN'T COME! I CAN'T COME!"

Jane made headlines across the country.

DESPERATE HOUSEWIFE TURNS SERIAL KILLER

WOMAN KILLS 11 MEN IN 24 HOURS

'CRAIGSLIST JANE' SLAYS 11

Jane had met men, one after another, at motels, at their homes, and even in random parking lots.

All had failed her unwinnable scenario, and all met their deaths on the spot at the manic hands of Jane Loisel. She was found mentally unfit to stand trial and sentenced to live out her life in a locked ward.

◆

"How has she been?" Pinky asked the veteran nurse who led them back.

"Same as always."

They reached a metal-finished door with a massive steel lock. There was viewing window and they each took a turn peering inside.

◆

The nurses told one another stories of hearing sounds from inside Jane's cell—sounds of sexual rapture. They liked to think she got some release, somehow, if only through her imagination. Jane spoke only one phrase anymore, to herself, to her rare visitors, to the nurses, to the cracks in the faux leather of her padding. One phrase echoed in her mind and through the halls of the institution, shook the dust from the rafters, and rang in the ears of those who came near.

"Ride . . . me home . . . to Hell . . . you resplendent stallion!"

3

Flowers at Funerals

Funerals are filled with paradoxes. We wear all black and leave white flowers. We try to focus on the happy times but the memories only make us sad. We ponder simultaneously life's brevity and the reality of forever. Love becomes loss and loss becomes love. At times of death, we express emotions we might never allow ourselves to release otherwise. In memory, saints become sinners, sinners become saints. Flowers are a felicitous symbol of this inner struggle, as they blossom outward.

Flowers are life and love, joy to the senses. When the snow melts, people await them as an age-old first sign and smell of rebirth. As varied and beautiful as humanity, flowers inspire us. With their pistils and stamens and pollen and exquisitely alluring petals, flowers are sex. From the decay of dirt, they sprout and flourish until cut.

Yet, the flowers piled on a casket or adorning a gravesite are as dead as what lies beneath them. Every cut flower has been dealt a mortal wound;

from the snipping of the shears, its countdown begins. How honest, then, for flowers at a funeral to be half-wilted! You can put them in a vase and fill them with chemicals to preserve their appearance, but the damage has been done. It's irreversible. A vase is a casket. Plant food, formaldehyde.

Life is all we know and all we have. All we can think to do with a dead body is bury it under soil. Six feet seems excessive, but we have our reasons. What if we were to see the body again, transformed in decay? Better to bury it below roots and rodents. Or burn it away until there's no trace of humanity, just sterile, unrecognizable ash. Or cast it into water. Anything so we can be sure we'll never see it devolve. That sight would be more than we could bear; the smell would be worse.

It is the flowers—still fragrant after being severed from their own hearts—that we call upon to save us!

◆

Life would not be what it is without death. Flowers show us that, too. Just as every sensational petal has a duller underside, death is surely the poignant counterpart to the joy that is life.

Go visit your loved ones where they sleep

dreamlessly; lay down your bouquet at your own feet, two meters above their heads. Let flowers be your ambassador. Hand pick your bouquet to chariot your sentiments to that other side. Surely, as you watch them withering and decaying right in front of you, they must somehow be blooming fresh in another realm, for your loved one's eyes.

While you sit, full of bittersweet emotion, look around you. Look at the grass and bushes and trees. Lean your head in, let your eyes soften and fill yourself with the smells of life. Maybe, just maybe, you'll see some flowers growing wild, blooming for you alone. Perhaps these flowers were cut dead on that other side. Perhaps your loved one is leaving them for you.

4

The Ode of Rust Wolf

I love you so dear, I'd kill any deer,
sang Rust Wolf to his mate.
For sakes of life and also fear;
our family's fragile fate.

Though shepherd staves and farmer guns
so sorely seek my death,
never will I slow my run
with prey blood on my breath.

For they all see my steely fur,
ore-orange stained so red,
and decry this soulless cur
of metal heart and head.

I can't deny titanium-strong
thoughtfulness of mind.
I kill to live my whole life long
and never glance behind.

But in my heart warm blood belies
my oxidized façade.
Surrounded by my pack, my eyes
swell with the love of God.

So through it all, I shall not shy,
I cannot change my tack.
When killing's done, love lives, and I
will not let starve my pack.

5

Modern Zombie

I'm alive but I'm dead.

I wake up every morning in my suburban bed, kiss my trophy wife, pat our his-and-hers kids on the head, stuff some name-brands in my mouth, and get in my minivan. On the way to my cubicle, I stop at the drive-thru for coffee. My life revolves around not losing these things. I have them now and I'm determined to keep them.

Every week, I go out to dinner with my folks. I bring them news, let them know that things are as good as they were seven days ago. It keeps them interested in me, I suppose, and keeps my choices validated. They approve. I pick up every check—it's nothing. What I tell them barely varies every week. They dote on their grandkids, though it's not quite how they doted on me when I was young.

I'm alive but I'm dead.

My parents are proud of me, of course. My house has one more bedroom than theirs does, and one more bathroom. We live one suburb away from them, in a better part of town.

As a child, I ran through the halls of our house, sides closing in. Dad tried to save space, Mom tried to save time. The house was full to bursting; they wanted it all, but could barely swing it. They both smelled of black coffee. I'm glad I'm still close by so I can visit them as they get older.

For them, growing up was tough. I had it so much better. They gave me this house by giving me the chance to afford it. They sent me to college, making sure my degree would be lucrative. I'm blessed to have been theirs, for who knows how I might've ended up? Certainly not with all this bounty. It's a good thing they took an interest in me, and a good thing I listened to them.

"There's no money in Marine Biology," they said. "Computers are the way to go." Off I went to the Institute of Technology. Now I have papers, a purebred's pedigree. I have my paperwork hanging on my cubicle half-wall so my boss can see it and remember why he hired me. Without the other two-and-a-half half-walls, the half-wall holding my degree would fall and crush me. Sometimes I think about it as I sit there. But at least I can afford a houseful of wife-and-kids.

I forget what my degree is in. Bachelor of Science in Paycheck? I could do my job in a coma. My arms and hands could just rely on muscle memory to keep clacking away at mouse and keyboard long after brain activity ceased, like the twitching of a squished spider's leg.

The only thing I need to change from workday to workday is my tie. Easy. I couldn't get fired if I wanted to—but why would I? I make more money than my dad ever did. I'm building a 401(k).

I'm alive but I'm dead.

My student loans were paid off exactly on time. I get promotions and benefits to keep me complacent. I wear flat-front khakis and drive a car that impresses people before they meet me. That is, when I'm not driving the minivan with the three-in-one infant travel system that my wife insisted on.

My parents and everybody else love my wife. Her roots never show and her cheekbones are perfectly even. She has white teeth like an angel. She's smart but not too smart, and always makes a good first impression, the one that lasts. She always wears the most flattering bras. All my buddies were jealous when I first started fucking her. We met over craft beer and Chardonnay, in a trendy bar near my business district. I was on my lunch hour, she was taking a break from shopping. We really connected. She asked me what car I drove, I asked her age, and we both approved of the answers.

I bought her dinner that night and found the conversation comfortable enough. I chased her smiles like a drug. After many dates and a few arguments, she told me her favorite color was yellow. The morning after, we both needed coffee.

I'm alive but I'm dead.

We co-signed in together. Down in the basement we have a wine cellar and a beer fridge. It's easier that way. She made me throw away all my video games, I made her do humiliating sex stuff.

My parents said, "Don't lose her! She's a keeper!" I bought a big, fat diamond. It took months to get her to say yes, but my parents were persistent. They wanted me to be happy. I wanted happiness, too, didn't I? Eventually, my parents talked to her parents and she realized she wanted to be happy, too.

I can still remember being in a rented tuxedo, at the wedding rehearsal, beside my best friend making obscene gestures about the shape of my fiancee's butt. It's been so long, now. Sometimes I forget what her skin smells like while she's out refilling her Valium prescription. My wife's practiced smile makes you want to smile even when there's nothing to smile about.

I'm alive but I'm dead.

With nothing better to do, we started trying for kids within a year. It took some doctoring, but we made sure to have one son and one daughter for the sake of our Christmas cards. We bought robin's-egg blue for our son, carnation pink for our daughter, and kept our fence white as paint. It's the old red-white-and-blue, just paler.

You have to tell your kids they can be anything. You have to tell them that money doesn't buy happiness. I tell them they live in the Land of the Free. They share their dreams with me.

When I drop my son off at hockey or pick up my daughter at her equestrian club, I remind them how lucky they are. My parents couldn't afford skates or stabling fees for me. I'm happy to pay now for what I can afford, but they need to know. Only by working all their lives as I have will they be able to provide as I can. They should be as successful as I am—no, more successful! They're able to do anything because I can provide it for them.

I go to their teacher conferences and negotiate their grades. They'd better start building a record for college now. What can they do without a degree? Who will pay them? It's as much a fact of life as conception. As sure as the rising sun, they need paychecks. Because the sky's the limit!

Watching their progress, I feel a satisfaction inflated with pure oxygen. I love them dutifully. I stir the aspartame into my coffee and wait for the caffeine to kick in.

I'm alive but I'm dead.

Every week, after dinner, I sit surrounded by pacified family. My parents, my children, my wife, and I, all digesting, contemplating whether we have room for dessert. We always do. Stuffed full, we exchange sighs as signs of how satisfied we all are with our decisions. The adults sip their coffee and the children smell it and ask for some.

"Just a sip," I say. "This is for grownups. It'll keep you awake." I let them try it unsweetened, to discourage them from developing a bad habit.

Afterward, home in bed, I dimly wish I'd ordered decaf. Something about lying awake after all the lights are off and the whole family is asleep makes my eyes float in tears. After enough time has passed, I slip into the bathroom with my new iPad to jerk myself off.

I think about my life on another timeline. I would be on a research boat in the Bahamas or the Gulf of Thailand, trying to untangle the world's mysteries and further human knowledge, leading a marine biology expedition for a university. My wife wouldn't have a made-up face but a genuine soul. I'd have met her on an expedition when we were both grad students. She would challenge me every day to be the best I could be. Her beauty might be harder for friends and parents to see, but hers would be a beauty immune to cellulite and wrinkles. When we made love, her orgasms wouldn't be an act. We would buy a small house that'd be empty half the year while we worked at our passions. We would home-school our only child on the boat, but make sure to enroll him or her in a school with friends when on land. Or, maybe we'd have no children.

My parents would whinge that they never saw us, that we were always out of cell range. I'd drive the same rust bucket for twenty-five years. Every day would be a floating vision. I'd have no retirement plan and would admit to myself that I hated coffee. I'd drink hot chocolate instead.

I'd be...alive?

My credit score is over 800. My wife's friends are jealous of my paychecks. My accountant promises me that I will be comfortable when I retire. My children will be respectable sources of pride.

My mom shows pictures of me, my wife, and the kids to her widow friends. On weekends I return to my dad's favorite church and watch his favorite football team on TV. My dog is a khaki-colored retriever. I'm at Starbucks before the sun is up. Every check clears.

I'm already dead.

6

A Walk Through Everything Fucking Falls State Park

One too-bright, grey morning I finally decided to wander the forest, looking for a tree. Not a tree to save, nor to live in. And not a tree to meditate under, like some seeker of enlightenment. I was looking for a tree that would serve my solitary purpose. It's hard to explain. I walked for fifteen minutes before so much as glancing up. I knew my tree wouldn't be easy to find. I longed to lose myself in leaves.

As I walked, I muttered fragments of full sentences running möbiusly around my freshly wounded mind. I mouthed a name.

You can walk through the woods for hours without a single tree catching your eye. I remembered my years in Boy Scouts, learning about shapes of leaves, textures of bark, hazards to avoid. *Most of the things I've been taught by someone else, I've forgotten shortly after the test.*

Striped maple. That one stuck with me. I learned that, to foresters and park rangers, the species is a weed. *I like striped maples.* True to their name, they wear pinstripes up their trunk. Juvenile striped maples, such as those I encountered, also have the industrial quality of making excellent walking sticks, straight and sturdy by nature. Their distinctive leaves give the tree its other name: goose-foot maple. *I guess I remember the interesting bits.*

Like many humans before me, I callously cut a stave for myself, separating it from its roots and branches. *I've only recently learned not to care.* It was still a bit bendy and whippy, with life at its core but, left to dry for a season or two, it would harden. I really do love the natural world, and I've learned of late that the proper word for what I am is hypocrite. What can I say? I longed for a companion.

My lungs filled with fresh-made oxygen and I simpered up at the canopy, to the rainclouds passing nearer. I distantly hoped they might have something for me before they dissipated to the south.

I couldn't help but laze around the first stream I encountered. The mourning doves had quieted for the day and the water's trickle cut through the soft breeze-rustle pleasurably. I gazed hard at the water, begging some crayfish or amphibian to make it's presence known to me. *I'm easily distracted like that. I wish I knew bird calls.* Downstream, I chanced to glimpse a solitary deer and I blinked a few extra times, suddenly muddled and out-of-place again. I wanted to do three different things.

I wanted to make easy eye-contact with the deer, tiptoe slowly, to be privileged with stroking the light-toast fur of its neck, and whispering a name into its ear.

I wanted my striped maple walking stick to have a hand-shaped stone fastened to its tip with the sinew of another deer. I would hunt my prey with it, as my paleolithic ancestors called out to me to do.

I wanted to leave, to scare the deer away purposely and walk back to safety and civilization. Then I would never stray back into this realm too simple for me to comprehend. But I had my purpose. The deer stepped away as I sat there, and I shed two tears.

In retrospect, I wanted to have done one other, utterly impossible thing: to share the sight with someone. *But it's too late, now.* My fists absorbed the wetness at my eyes.

I decided it was a good time to leave the stream and go further.

For a while again, no trees mattered. I must've been beneath some oaks, since my off-brand Timberlands began kicking acorns. I found a fat one and removed its cap so I could amuse myself with a trick I knew. Holding it between my thumbs and blowing across its cavity, I produced a shriek.

It sounds like youth in unbridled desperation.

Like an apex predator, I let myself be loud without care, smiling at my own obnoxiousness and listening for the thin echo. I then cached away the little noisemaker for later and continued through an autumn's worth of acorns, my footsteps occasionally startling some squirrel or chipmunk like a snap-trap.

Without fanfare, the rain arrived. *It's louder in the forest.* The drops meet the canopy leaves, then the bush-and-sapling leaves, and finally hit bottom. *It can still seem like it's pouring long after the clouds are gone.*

I skipped under the umbrella of a weeping willow, grinning like heartbreak in denial. I resisted a carnal craving to carve initials into the trunk. *Who'd ever see them?* I resolved to wait beneath its wind-washed foliage. Sitting, I watched the rain falling through a window frame of willow fronds. I took out my little acorn shell again, and this time its shriek was all but drowned out by the raucous water. I cackled without joy.

Above me, wrens darted all ways impatiently, never satisfied with their current twig. *How perfectly one might fit into my own cupped hands. How easily I could destroy it then. I could love it or destroy it. The worst would be to do both.*

I pulled a pack of cigarettes from my pocket and sucked bitter menthol. *This is the perfect time for a churchwarden's pipe full of loose-leaf tobacco.* I yearned again for a long-obsolete time. Smoking and lounging for the duration of the storm, I envisioned a lazy summer hurricane instead of an October noon shower. A few placid drops reached my face to wash it. For the only time in my life, I did not litter my butts. *I've done enough.*

The rain reached that ethereal point where I couldn't tell if it was still coming from the clouds or just idly gravitating from leaves. I ventured deeper.

Along an easy slope, a grove of aspens formed sparse columns. Ahead of their surrounding neighbors, their leaves were already changing colors and starting to fall. I was washed in fiery briskness. Beneath the amber of the aspens, not much grew besides small clumps of grasses. Their exposed roots provided a tripping hazard, and more than once I depended on my walking stick. The aspens reminded me of paper bark birches and I rued the reality. *There's a comfort in paper.*

I don't know why, but I expected the ground in that particular area to be littered with browning pine needles despite no present evergreens. They would've fit my scene.

I checked my cell and smirked. Even for all my lost rambling, I still had service. Hell, I still had 4G. I wanted a pokey blue spruce to come into existence near me to throw the thing against. I envisioned the phone's logos and screen pierced through with pine needles, like a boar in a trou-de-loup, bleeding liquid crystal. I sank the device back into my pocket, trying to forget what time and date the screen had displayed. *It's the present, nothing's changed that.*

I left the aspens, still dressed in their golden hue, and realized the sun was setting. I hadn't had a bite or drink since the night before. My stomach murmured occasionally but that particular discomfort paled and I continued to ignore it.

I thought I might've found what I was looking for in an ash tree. Standing at its base and looking up, I could feel something. Maybe it was the future. I've heard we can't live without trees.

They're only installed for decoration of course, usually after the naturally occurring trees have been razed. It's a lot of work.

The house I grew up in had a small, unfenced front yard that ended at the sidewalk. Between the sidewalk and the street was a small plot of grassy weeds with a tree in the middle—I couldn't tell you what variety. The patch of grass looked like it belonged to us, and we mowed it, but it was the city's property. One year, city workers came and spray-painted an orange 'X' on the trunk of that tree. It was as if they had a file on that tree and had condemned it by secret tribunal.

A week or so later, some other city employees came out and sawed the tree to a stump. *I guess the branches had leaned too far out into the road for their comfort.* Another month or whatever later, still more city workers came and extracted as much of the stump as they could. The next spring, they planted a new sapling on the same spot, like a D.I.Y. phoenix. Alongside the sapling, they stuck two dead wooden stakes and tied them to the young tree with wire. They wanted to make damn sure this one would grow up straight.

I presume at some point our collective laziness will take over and we won't be bothered to replace the ones that inconvenience us. *I hope I'm dead before that comes to pass.*

While standing in my spot under the mighty boughs of the ash, I saw a future where that pitiful tree gets cut down, and this time, a new one isn't worth planting. Or the tree dies. *Or I kill the tree.*

I had lived in a city, yet the trees were what I remembered about my street. Four seasons of beautiful wilderness lined up mathematically.

I shook my head, dismissing the ash to blow in the wind.

The sun left a little twilight to guide me further into the forest. I waxed melancholic, disdaining the life around me. This, in turn, tinged me with guilt. In just-before-darkness, I stretched my shoulders and my hand encountered the trunk of a tree. Due to lack of lighting and learning, I decided rather randomly that it was a sycamore. I leaned, with a sigh as heavy as the world, against its trunk and strained my arms, questioning.

My right hand encountered a low branch. Desperately, I wrapped my fingers around it and began to pull myself up. An owl silently fluttered past my eyes nearby, but I couldn't stop climbing, first six feet, then two stories from the ground. I hugged the trunk and continued ascending into darkness.

I remembered climbing trees as a kid, always afraid to go too high, fretting about how I'd get down. Classmates I knew had broken limbs falling from trees. *Going up seems smoother than going down, and more hopeful, even if it's a dead end. Every tree is a fun adventure to a child. He will try to climb any tree that has strong branches within reach. Even an overgrown bush will suffice.*

Sweat bit into my eyes as I climbed, but I dared not spare a hand, wrist, elbow, or shoulder to wipe it away. I pulled myself higher than I had ever allowed myself to do as a youngster. If my mother could see me now, she would be distraught, screaming for my return to sanity.

But I'm already so far!

I didn't look around and I didn't look out. I just kept hauling myself higher. Panting and reckless, I finally poked my head up above the canopy and saw only what there was.

How small I felt—merely an annoyance—in the tree, in the grove, in the forest, in the state, in the world, in the middle of the cosmos.

I breathed deeply the optimistic night air. The dark of the forest floor and the serenity of the forest canopy glimmered, two sides of night's black lucky coin. *I love this time, between the stars and leaves.* I wouldn't-couldn't look down. Surely a fall from so great a height would dash me out of life. I stood on the tree's crown like cut obsidian, balancing for hours, breathing and loving.

Over and over, my lips mouthed the rote syllables of a name I was unable to sound.

Around me, the nocturnal animals went about their surviving unheeded. Some far-off wolf howled and I couldn't resist replying as best I could. To him, I'm sure I had a strange accent. I hope he wasn't offended. *That's the way I think.* It's a skill I wish I could read a technical blog about: howling.

I imagined myself falling, breaking my neck, the wolf following my weird call out of curiosity. *He would make a meal of my carrion, share me with his whole pack, and they'd live another few days. Maybe one would break a tooth on my cursed cellphone. The alpha male and female would eat the good meat, feed their cubs my very best bits. Coyotes would fight over the Genuine Leather in my shoes. Buzzards and bugs would leave me clean.*

I stood at the top of my supposed sycamore for so long that pink started creeping up on the horizon. I felt the breezes running through me.

The warm coolness of nature welled up from my numbing toes, through my aching calves and thighs, past my protesting stomach, into my chest full of broken pieces. It possessed my mouth and finally moistened my eyes so that they became clear and empty with purpose. I howled again, hoping the coming dawn couldn't yet hear me and would leave me alone. I smiled a smile much wider than my coping-mechanism smile.

"I'm coming," I whispered, then howled again and screamed a name so awesomely loud it tore my throat.

I jumped.

7

Eye of the Beholder
An essay

I don't really fear death. Through half a dozen or so funerals I've attended in twenty-six years, plus one grandfather dead on (my) arrival into this world, even at this age, I see death, well...like it's cliché counterpart, taxes: godawful, utterly unavoidable, but nothing to fear. I'm assuming fear will come, if at all, when I'm older and sense that I'm closer to it. I can tell you that watching my wife's liver fail has forced me to respect death. As if facing the Sovereign of the Realm, I have had to bow my head and kiss its ring and scrape my forehead at its feet, circumventing what I thought to be courage in its face.

At the time of this writing, I still don't have any conclusive word on whether my wife will survive or perish. Her hospital room is a limbo on Earth where we await damnation or salvation. All I can do is watch as my mind spirals outward.

Death seems black and white, like an on-off switch, and to its subject, that's not wrong.

But in the eye of the beholder, death can be like beauty. Shades of color paint every death we know uniquely.

The death of my grandfather, the one I never knew, who died before I lived, somehow tints my life the faintest translucent brown, like sunlight through smog you can sense but not see. Something subconscious surely developed in my psyche because of his death, although I was not yet even a concept when it happened. Perhaps that innate knowledge of death contributes to my present fascination with the subject.

My other grandfather died in my late adolescence, and yes, I was sad. Sad is probably the best word. Not morose. My grief came primarily secondhand from my dad and other family members, people who make a point of keeping their feelings from showing. The truth is, he died slowly, over months if not years, well into his nineties. How could I be surprised?

His death shone beige. I did love him as one learns to love a relative, and enjoyed his cheery disposition. But for some deaths—like his—one has the chance to prepare emotionally. At least I think so. It's all subjective.

When my wife's grandfather died from Alzheimers, the real sadness came from the horrid nature of the disease he'd suffered. That, and seeing my distraught lover in mourning. Hers were the happy memories of a massive garden along Black Creek and a special bond between two souls separated by a generation but bound by metaphysical blood. I saw his death in pallid blue.

I had an aunt who died from a long battle with muscular dystrophy when I was very young. Her death came prematurely, but also not. She lived many states away. If I went to the funeral, I have no memories of it because of my age, and because it came around the same time as another death that was weightier to my family: that of my paternal grandmother. The aunt's mother.

The aunt's death seemed almost an afterthought, a faint shade of white, tinged hospital green. My grandmother's seemed gilded and substantial. She also lived out of town—I barely knew her—and she'd been fading from cancer; but the end came at my kin like a boxing glove hidden inside a jack-in-the-box.

Her heirlooms hold places of reverence in my parents' house, reviving the sentiments people have always associated with her. As I said, I barely knew her. I met her just once or twice. Yet, her death is the golden one. I guess that's how I learned to behold it.

I would call the death of my great aunt my first close-up glimpse at death. She was in declining health for all of the time I was alive and cognizant. But, of course, I already knew what death was by then; I was a teen. Perhaps her physical condition and my innate understanding of death kept me from forming close bonds with her, since, when she died, I wasn't particularly moved. It seemed... natural. She was old and infirm and death is what happens to the old and infirm. The event only confirmed my assumptions about the scientific nature of death, and was my first clearly memorable experience of witnessing the incomprehensible mourning of others. Not so much a color per se, I would describe her death to me as clear.

My wife was the only reason I attended—and even served as a pallbearer—at my uncle-in-law's chartreuse funeral. Of the man, I knew only the evil things he had purportedly done. I had to suppress surprise when people seemed grief-stricken. From everything I'd heard, he'd left behind a lot of burnt bridges and suffering. But death must be respected. I didn't understand that then.

Maddy's death hit me the hardest of those that I've experienced. My wife and I called her Aunt, despite there being no blood relation. She officiated at our wedding, and it feels wrong to call such a person anything but family. Her death rolled all the way across the country in a thunderous wave of disturbing crimson.

Grieving is for the life lost, and her life truly felt the most like a loss. Perhaps that's why I haven't grieved for family members the way I grieved for her; I just didn't know them well enough to grieve.

Anyway, I think it's less about grieving than respect. Death requires a tithe, if not of grief then of respect, as surely as taxes. Even the suicide bomber who pushes the button in a crowd represents a life lost to his loved ones—just as his victims do. All deaths must be respected in some way.

It took my wife's diagnosis to pound that into me. Even a few days of contemplating the possibility of losing such a life created respect where previously existed none.

My wife's death will be pure black whenever it comes. That is, black as defined by the absence of all color rather than the combination of all colors. Black as a night when you can't sleep. Black like all you can see with your face buried sobbing in a pillow.

Maddy left behind a lover, too. As I contemplate the prospect of my wife's mortality, I know that I can't know the anguish Maddy's lover suffered at her passing. But for once, I can begin to imagine it, with my wife away from home in hospital care, waiting to see if her coin will land on heads or tails.

If you've never been forced to respect death, you can't comprehend future pain brought to the present. When you care about a life, death shows you exactly how much, and what you stand to lose. You can't picture a future scene without a hole in it. You can't see having fun without that pang in your sternum reminding you of how that fun might've been shared with a person who made everything extra fun just by being there. When the life of someone you loved has concluded, the future changes from color to sepia-tone.

The next time you introduce yourself, it will be as a widower or a widow, not a husband or wife. Your dinner reservations will no longer be for two. Who knows how many years it will be before you kiss another pair of lips? If ever? Where you once imagined a future as part of an old couple with well-worn smile wrinkles that tug every time somebody tells you how inspirational your love is, you instead envision a future where everyone at your nursing home tries to avoid your sour mug and stone-carved frown lines. You wonder if you can survive to old age alone.

At past memorials, I was naive, cocky, and callous. Now I respect death.

It strikes me as poetry without beauty that the name of the organ that may kill her is "liver."

I feel the grip of death's hand bending my neck, shoving me to my knees, forcing me prostrate onto the cold, dirty ground. Death itself is not cold. Death is the absence of any of that kind of sensation. It takes away the ability to feel anything but empty, hollow loss.

Some deaths roll past us and we're fine. Some deaths cause less stress than an impending deadline at work. Some deaths make us reflect and emerge as better people. Some deaths are less...loss. Some deaths create fallout that's worse than the detonation. Some deaths, we're too young to understand. Some deaths, we don't feel able or allowed to mourn. Some deaths barely make a blip on our radar.

But death—all death—must be respected. If you love someone, you know this. Or you will, one day.

Unbroken

Happy birthday, Great Grandma!
Happy birthday to you!

♦

"Thank you all!" she said, as countless orange candle flames reflected mirth in her spectacles. "How warm it is, and how lucky I am! Four generations all in one room! Come here, my little great grandson, my greatest, grandest achievement. Come sit on my lap. It's still vigorous enough for growing tykes. Not much is notable about my life, besides it's length. I didn't invent some new "o-matic" and my name never appeared on a marquee. I was never best at a thing—or worst, for that matter. I made no waves and started no movements. I built nothing up nor tore anything down. I contributed nothing but all of you.

"I know I can't take it all, but I do feel due a sum of credit. Look at you all! So many smiling faces that might not have been! So many laughs and tears we've shared in various combinations of together! It is such an earthly blessing to know you all, and to know I had a hand in bringing your brightness into this world!

"With all its flaws and worries and troubles and fears, the world was meant for you. I may be a simple old-timer, but all I ask for is this life surrounding me. I love you all so much—as well as those who will follow you, those I will never meet, those who have not yet come out to experience the seasons. Please tell them when they get here that I love them just as I love you."

With that, she sat gently and watched the candles burn down as her family all reflected.

◆

"Greah grammah?" the ignorant tot cooed from her lap.

"Yes?" Wisdom looked down at him, wrinkled and frail.

"Iz thera greah grampah?"

"You do have a great grandpa, tender one. But I'm sad to share that he is dead, and has been since before you were born. Death is a natural part of life."

"Oh. Can I meet him?"

"Only in pictures and stories. Once somebody is dead, you can't meet them in person anymore."

"Greah Grammah?"

"Yes?" Their eyes met, his clouded with confusion, hers clear with tears.

"What's 'dead?'"

Before she could blow them out herself, the candles snuffed; the child spooked reflexively.

9

Consumption

People didn't like Danvil but Danvil liked people. As a schoolboy, he'd been awkward and covered with greasy zits. Even with thick glasses to assist his sight, he constantly bumped into things and knocked over breakables. His voice was grating, nasal and staccato, abrading even the most tolerant listeners' patience. His smile turned others' into grimaces. It was a losing battle to get anyone to hold his gaze.

Born with an intestinal condition, Danvil took medicine every day that came with an unfortunate side effect. His body exuded the smell of stale bread. Born to exhausted parents with more children than funds to provide for them, he grew up wearing hand-me-downs of indiscriminate size and gender. He started balding before he was twenty. Yet, Danvil endured it all with a storm-beaten smile.

The closest thing Danvil found to a friend went by the name of Morana. All of Morana's friends had drifted away, partly due to the post-high-school diaspora to colleges, but mostly because she had started exhibiting signs of paranoid schizophrenia. Morana and Danvil had graduated in the same class and enrolled in the same community college. In each other, they found someone who would not be scared away. His smile, his smell, his small personality made her feel safe in the eye of a hurricane of hallucinatory sights and sounds. He drove her to doctors and pharmacists when her friends and family didn't care to make the time.

When Morana went off her meds at age twenty-six and disappeared, Danvil was the one on the front lines searching and leaving frantic messages on cell phones, all of which were dismissed to voicemail after two rings. He found her in their favorite place in the world, a park on the edge of town called "The Poet's Garden," full of willows and lilac bushes and a stream that fed a marsh. Morana had taught Danvil to do yoga there. She and he had visited there often, to feel the silence, to hear and see peace.

Her body was a downward-facing dog by the slow stream. Beside her on the bank rested a razor blade smeared with a dried, black hint of what had transpired. She'd opened her wrists and drained them away into the marsh.

Something about the bite marks on Morana's toothsome legs—probably left by some coyote— made Danvil realize he was starving. Rather than alert the authorities to his discovery, he waited as darkness fell and then left silently— with Morana.

Back in his cramped, one-room apartment, he tasted for the first time—a soul. No kiss nor love-spurred tongue's caress, but a baser mouthful. In the chewing, Danvil realized that, despite her death, Morana could still be with him.

"Oh, Morana, you're just as sweet as I've always imagined! Truly a treat, I'm honored! It's sad you can't taste yourself. You know, you've shown me what we've both been too afraid to say out loud. You love me. And, of course, I love you! You knew that all along, didn't you?"

For the first time in his life, Danvil spoke without stuttering, his vocal cords ringing with deep confidence.

The next day, he shaved his head clean, doing away with the male-pattern hairline he'd always hated. Reading the paper over a breakfast of Morana on toast, he noticed an ad for a job as an assistant to an embalmer. It paid twice his grocery-stocker's salary. Danvil picked up the phone and surprised himself by securing an interview for the following Friday.

On the page opposite the embalmer's notice, a half-page ad for a suit sale caught his eye and he hopped the bus downtown. The clothing displayed in the store's window looked so dashing that Danvil figured it must be well outside his meager budget. But the ad had promised bargains, so in he strode.

As he crossed the threshold, confetti cascaded all around him. Cheery calliope music started up and a banner popped down from the ceiling. The store's enthusiastic owner rushed toward him with several managers in tow: he was their one-millionth customer. In a whirl, he found himself standing in front of a three-way mirror, tape measures flying. He was the lucky winner of a new suit, custom made for him from decadent European fabrics. His smile finally began to look appropriate on his face.

As he sat down for his interview at the funeral home, before he'd even uttered a word, he knew he had the job. He couldn't wait to run home and tell Morana the good news!

Dinner, however, turned bittersweet. Danvil realized the provisions of Morana's body were running out. After hacking off whatever he could salvage, he carried what was left of her back to the Poet's Garden for a proper burial. He scattered lilac seeds over her plot in lieu of a tombstone and cursed his poverty. He would have loved to bury her within the confines of a backyard fence he didn't own.

◆

It took some time to adjust to his new line of work. Seeing so much life cut short taxed his senses and his emotions. He learned about faces—how to reconstruct and repair them, how they look under the light. The customers cared deeply about the faces and demanded perfection, regardless of the circumstances, all for that last glance into an open casket before shutting it forever.

One day, a man came onto the slab who looked familiar to Danvil. They had met when they were boys. Larry Jones, Danvil recalled. Larry was always inviting friends over to use his parents' pool or play expensive video games. Danvil had always hoped, quite in vain, to be invited over one day. After studying the boy, now a man, now a corpse—he looked around to make sure that he was alone. Then, he sawed off Larry's inanimate left foot, wrapped it in aluminum foil, and threw it in the back of the employee freezer.

At home, Danvil fried strips of Larry in a pan for dinner.

"Wow! Talk about flavor! I'm glad you decided to come over and hang out, Larry, I've always thought you were a really cool guy! Yes, of course I forgive you for those wedgies—already forgotten! I really think this is the start of a life-long friendship!"

The next morning, Danvil slunk into work easing back dread. His boss would already be pumping the preserving fluids into the remainder of Larry's body and as soon as they started squirting out of the left ankle, Danvil's actions would be unhideable.

"Danvil," his boss began, as soon as he walked in. "I need to ask you something."

He gulped down anxiety. "Yes, sir?"

"How would you like to finish embalming and preparing Mr. Jones by yourself?"

"What?"

"I've been watching you and you've made genuine progress since you started here. I want you to show me what you can do without any help. What do you say?"

"Absolutely, sir! I'll make you proud!"

So of course, he did. Delighted at the chance to prove himself and cover up his proclivity,

Danvil set about the task with gusto. And, unable to resist, he harvested a bit more protein before spoiling the rest with formaldehyde.

"Excellent job, Danvil, great attention to detail!" said his boss upon examination of his effort. "You filled in the bullet holes flawlessly and he looks like he dressed himself! The family will be delighted. I knew you had it in you!" He paused for effect, then said, "Danvil, my boy?"

"Yes?"

"There's something you should know. I'm moving the funeral home. Business has been booming and I found a new space downtown. There'll be work for an additional full-time embalmer and the job's yours, if you want it. Mr. Jones in there was a test of sorts. Needless to say, you aced it. I'll still be your boss, of course, but you'll have your own room. You'll do all your own preservations from start to finish. The position comes with a sizable raise and, within reason, you can make your own schedule. What do you say?"

◆

"Morana! Larry! I'm home! I just got a promotion—me!" Danvil chattered about his exquisite work that day. "You would be proud, man, I made you look like a million bucks! I should thank you, really, because I got this new gig because of you! Wow, what great friends we make!"

With more money coming in, Danvil soon bought himself a house—an updated colonial out in the suburbs. With four bedrooms and three bathrooms, it sounded unnecessarily spacious to his buyer's agent, but Danvil didn't want his friends to feel crowded.

Thanks to Danvil's new responsibilities and freedom, more and more people—well, chunks of them, anyway—ended up on Danvil's plate. The pastor from his childhood church turned up on his slab one day, dead from autoerotic asphyxiation. Danvil carefully applied makeup and putty to remove the blue tinge and ligature marks from the pastor's skin, to preserve the serene visage for his mourners. Then he filleted the man's meaty calves and thighs and masked the wounds with the cleric's robes provided by his wife.

The next day before work, Danvil faced his own face in the mirror and decided to grab his makeup kit. Skillfully, he blended away his acne scars and brightened his sunken eyes. He took off his glasses and scowled at the blurry sight. A growing sense of self love welled up from deep in his gut, and he sat down at his computer to open Google.

After some hasty searching, he picked up the phone and called out sick from work. Then, he made an appointment with a laser surgeon. Over the course of an afternoon—a blink of an eye in his long-bespectacled life—Danvil found himself no longer encumbered with awkward, thick glasses.

Conversing idly with the surgeon after the procedure, he learned about a new medicine that had come out in recent months to treat just the sort of congenital intestinal trouble he'd dealt with all his life—with no strange-scented side effects. The same day, he called his gastro-enterologist for a prescription.

◆

The following Friday night, Danvil put on his custom suit in front of a full-length mirror while making an announcement to Morana, Larry, Pastor Roberts, and several other friends he'd consumed of late. He was going out. Once again, he made up his face.

In a wine bar called Sky Blue, he successfully chatted up women. Nobody avoided his gaze or made excuses to disengage with him. He natu-rally found words to say and his smile went viral.

That night, he went home with a woman:

Meera. The sun rose the following morning on a Danvil uncharacteristically ecstatic! Just the thought of Meera made Danvil sigh. She wore her hair straight and black, the last vestige of a high school goth phase that had included bondage pants and chain chokers. She read Fitch and Palahniuk and loved the fact that Danvil worked as an embalmer. Danvil could never have imagined his fortune! Finally he was able to say he'd found someone; he had a girlfriend!

"I think I'm ready to meet your roommates, Danvil." Meera began, one day some months into their relationship. "I know you said it's complicated or whatever, but I don't care. I've never been to your place and I think it'll be fine."

"Well, if you're sure, I guess it's OK. But you need to know that one of my roommates, we kind of dated and—to be honest—I think she still has feelings for me. But you don't need to worry about anything."

"Yes, you've told me all about it already. Let's just go over there, OK?"

They drove to Danvil's updated colonial in Meera's car and parked in the driveway. In seconds, he was pushing the door open to his empty house.

"Hi, everyone! Come meet Meera! This is the

girl I've told you all about!" Danvil called cheerfully, then grinned up into the silence.

"W-where is everyone?" Meera asked.

"Come on, don't be rude. Come in, say hi! This is Pastor Roberts, this is Margo, here's Morana, she's—" He pointedly caught Meera's eye and mouthed the words, ex-girlfriend. "Here comes Larry; Garret's here, too, and his wife Lacie and the twins, Micah and Seth. Don't be shy, shake hands! They're all lovely people!"

"Danvil..." Meera stepped backward into the doorframe and a cold-water sensation trickled down her spine.

"What is it?"

"Are your friends...imaginary?"

"What? Imaginary?! They're as plain as the nose on my face!" He pointed to himself, creating a hideous gouge in his thick makeup.

"What the hell is going on?"

"Meera! Just listen to me!" He tried to think back...to his meals...his meat in the fridge... Morana. His thoughts formed a heavy lump in his throat that tasted like bile. "No! Go away! If you don't like my friends, then I don't like you! They've been by my side through thick and thin, through good times and bad times, and they would take a bullet for me! Would you take a bullet for me, Meera?!"

Meera ran to the curb, and Danvil watched her black hair flutter as she fled. The tires shrieked as she sped away.

♦

The next day at work, Danvil worked on the class clown from his high school homeroom, the victim of a heroin overdose. Rather than embalming him, Danvil severed the head with a saw. After his boss went home, he took the entire body out to his car wrapped in a sheet. For the funeral the next day, he stuffed a suit with pillows and placed the head at the collar. The family didn't notice anything.

"We have a new friend, everyone! Morana, Larry, you might remember Lucas from high school? Oh right, Margo, I think he used to mow your lawn, too. He's still got the jokes! Tell 'em, Lucas, the one you told me on the way over here, about the nuns? Oh...wait. Pastor Roberts might get offended! Never mind—he said go ahead, he's heard 'em all!"

It was all very festive, but eating Lucas didn't ease a nagging doubt gnawing at the corners of Danvil's mind.

Morose, he took Thursday and Friday off from

work. He felt summoned to the Poet's Garden, and when he got there, he sat down among the lilacs. Until long after the sun disappeared, he lingered in contemplation. Around midnight, an epiphany broke over him.

"I'm so sorry, Morana!" He cried. "She meant nothing to me! I'll make it all better, just you wait!"

Fingernails clotted with grime, Danvil shoveled down under the lilacs, frantic to move the Earth away and find her. In tears, sweat, blood, and worms, he fumbled in the dark, not caring what he uncovered as he made his way toward her bones. He knew where to dig, of course, and although it would be impossible to locate every single piece of her in the dead of night, he piled up whatever he could find until he located the beloved skull that had once housed his favorite mind. He took the spoils to his suburban backyard and reburied them in a corner beneath a young alder. Maybe if he gave her a better resting place his mind would be at ease.

Back inside his kitchen, still muddy from head to toe, he gorged himself on Lucas.

First thing on the following Monday morning, Danvil's boss called him into his office.

"It's time," the older man began. "I've been thinking about this for a few months now, and

I'm ready to retire. I can't think of anyone I'd rather have succeed me than you. You're a gifted embalmer and you understand the business. I want to leave it all to you. How does that sound?"

"Like Heaven on Earth!" said Danvil eagerly. "I didn't know it before I took this job, but a dream is coming true for me right now!"

"I'm happy for us both, Danvil. I'll be leaving the first of the month. Drink?"

◆

For a while, Danvil distracted himself with running the business of death. He needed to hire three more people to do all the work his boss had been handling. The funeral home had an excellent reputation and, to Danvil's delight, people did die every day. Anytime the body on his slab belonged to someone he knew or admired or remembered from his life, he took a piece home—a grisly doggy bag.

His business flourished; he bought himself a Cadillac. His relationship with his friends, however, began to feel unnatural. One night, he woke up mucky with sweat.

"I've got it! I know how to fix everything! Morana, I know we've had our ups and downs, but I can make it all right! You wait here and I'll be back in a jiffy!"

Twenty minutes later, his Cadillac idled on the curb outside Meera's house.

Neighbors heard breaking glass and then screaming, and quickly called the police. Meera had to be rushed to a hospital. She needed skin grafts, blood transfusions, and a host of antibiotics to treat the numerous wounds where Danvil had gnashed off chunks of flesh from her living arms and legs.

In the back of a police car, Danvil sat shackled at the wrists and ankles. The officers had pulled his shirt up over his face so he couldn't chomp at them.

The judge accepted the insanity plea offered by Danvil's public defender and arrangements were made for him to be held in an asylum.

After he tried to eat his own arm, he had to be strapped to his bed twenty-four hours a day.

No one came to visit Danvil—but people visiting other patients heard him chattering away with nobody and assumed he suffered from severe schizophrenia.

But Danvil knew the truth. Even there, surrounded by sterile white and sickly green, subjected to daily injections, he kept smiling. All the friends and family he had ever needed or wanted lived on inside him, in his head, where everything was alive. They were all breathing, smiling, kissing, and hugging him and telling him all he ever wanted to hear: "You are loved."

My River

I fell with your water, from wild, where you
    flowed,
many mad midnights mooning o'er your melt-
    snow.

From high in the hill,
sure, she's Mountain's daughter.
How dry, there's a chill,
in her "please-love-me" water.
A shy, grown, young rill
playing free as her otter.
Oh, pine, do I still,
For the seas never caught her.

After you, I freefell, you flashed, fishes, a show.
You led, love, I followed: loam, lichen below.

Sweet prize of my eye,
steep ground, she descended,
and nighly, I cried,
as roundly, she bended.

Love, I now but sigh.
She wound and expended.
Please, why say goodbye?
No down delta, she's ended.

You never knew ocean, not near did you go.
Your blue bled to brown, your bright bubbles
        have slowed.

I now trudge bog
and dread-soaked black larches,
sigh-choking fog
and dead tree-limb arches.
My heart's cracked and clogged,
 my treads: lost in marshes.

Thigh-deep in sog,
my head-man still marches.

No more do we romp
                your
                        shore.
No stride, strut or stomp;
                    we've
                        cleft.
No funeral pomp
                    in
                        hoar.
No thing but a swamp
                    is
                        left.

Stigma

*C*RACK. "Guilty." The sound of the gavel sundered me. I couldn't hear the sentence over my own screaming disbelief and the family's cheers of relief. My lawyer warned me that, based on the charges, I would either go to jail for life or face death, a distinction that didn't matter. Only the perversion of lawfulness mattered.

That hammer crack tore through the judge's bench into the concrete below the industrial carpeting. That floor shattered away around me as I fell through the chasm into a prison cell where I'd spend all of the ever I had left.

My lawyer said we could appeal, but I doubt it will matter. You should've seen the scene the family made in court. They weren't there when it happened. They don't know what transpired. They just ache for their daughter, niece, granddaughter, cousin, friend. We all do. And yelling themselves hoarse at me in the courtroom must've soothed a fraction of their anguish.

"RAPIST!"

"KILLER!"

"Please! Listen to me—!" Even when the judge had called the court to order, a buzz clogged everyone's ears as I pleaded. My own children couldn't look me in the eye.

I had told them to check my DNA. They'd said a condom had been used. I had told them to put me in a lineup, but the witness had faltered.

"It was just too dark."

Inconclusive. I never let go of my innocence. At least I still have that, which is more than the victim can say.

They shoved evidence photos in front of me as if I was expected to recognize the lacerated, lifeless, little angel. My youngest child was the same age. The cops looked at my hands and knew those hands had destroyed clothing, flesh, life, virtue. They never even looked for other suspects. I threw up when they showed me the photos. They haunted my hope.

I can't get those photos to let me go. They're branded into my mind as surely as the inmate number on my jumpsuit, 24871, has been branded across my body. That will stay true even if I appeal and win. I cry in my cell, unable to escape any of it.

It's clear that I was never considered innocent, not from the very start. I first saw that in the arresting officer's eyes. He was just feeding an appetite born of such a moving crime. Such an atrocity leaves crowds of people feeling helplessly alone. It's a nightmare so real it inspires a dancing, glowing blackness, which I could see in the jurors' eyes. It's a perfectly rational response to such evil actions. But it provoked irrational overreaction in that courtroom.

I wonder about God more and more. Some of my fellow inmates say they've found God here, among all the grey. They tell me God has a special plan for me. If I'm innocent, I'll be redeemed—if not through the courts, then in Heaven. People make mistakes but God is perfect, all-knowing, all-powerful.

It's soothing, it really is, to feel such serenity in the face of perfect desolation. But that's more self-centered than I'm capable of being.

I've never been under any delusions as to why the jury, the prosecutor, the judge and the family all came to the same false conclusion. It was about humanity, fragility. I know how I look. They reacted instinctively, their fear sparking aggression. I stand six-foot-six. I was a linebacker in high school and college, until it interfered with other goals. My brow is low and thick over my eyes. Combined with my slumping posture, I have the appearance of an ogrish troll, larger than life. A monster. And monsters rape and kill six-year-old girls.

Prison has its own code of ethics. An eye for an eye has sounded fair before, a rape for a rape. Children are off limits to even the bloodiest Blood. My fellow prisoners have concluded that I deserve to be here beside them—maybe I deserve more. It's not hard for me to imagine the violence anyone would be capable of with justice for a child in mind.

Of course, I can fend off a testosterone-jacked rageaholic, even when cornered; that's why they come at me as a gang. Half a dozen or more multiple-murderers hold me down with muscle forged daily in the yard, each chasing a ravenous hunger spawned in a manmade interpretation of righteousness.

"I'm innocent, I sw—" is all I can get out before my words are crammed back in.

"You like rapin' little girls, pedo pervert?!"

"You gonna be our little girl tonight, bitch!"

The guards hear it. They figure I deserve it, too. And if the prisoners can vent their energy, they're more inclined to comply with commands.

Yet still, there is an unknown Nobody that is

my truest torment. Occasionally I've asked God about Nobody, the one never to be convicted, who obliterated that angel's life. He adjusts his rear-view mirror in brazen pride, never afraid of blue-and-red lights appearing behind him. Nobody will be more careful in the future, leave fewer clues. There will be more young innocents: a reptilian brain's conquests. But these won't make the news. There will be no mugshot of Nobody's face on *Channel Six at Six*, as there was of mine. Nobody's victims' families won't make newsreels, howling "CONVICT NOBODY! NOBODY IS SATAN! HOW COULD NOBODY DO THIS TO OUR LITTLE ANGEL?!"

While my jury and my D.A. and my judge all feel justice was served, Nobody's future victims will simply disappear. Their faces will crop up on milk cartons or in the back of the Pennysaver, or at Wal-Mart near the water fountains. Every few years, there will be an update to the digitally enhanced image of what they should look like today, as if they're alive.

Nobody will leave acid, gaping question-mark holes throughout the neighborhoods, in an outward spiral.

What does God have to say about him? I've never heard a satisfying answer. God will surely send him to Hell when he dies. But until then, Nobody will be free, full of that same rapture a pilot feels who spent a childhood gazing out windows. He has already realized his own Heaven on Earth. What does he care about Hell? He surely doesn't believe.

And so he'll kill another child who fits his type. Her mother, crushed under an avalanche of grief, will kill herself. Her father will pick up a bottle and then a pipe, lose his job, commit an armed robbery. In prison, he'll join a gang for protection and kill another inmate. He'll die with a sponge on his head wired to a scissor switch, in front of a handful of scowling faces.

Where will this mother and father go? To Heaven or to Hell? If the daughter was baptized, she's waiting for them in Heaven.

If the parents go to Hell, they may meet up with their child's killer and finally get some...closure? Justice? Revenge? Maybe they'll force him to disclose where their child was buried.

And as for me and God? Well, I could hoard away faith for myself, stockpile it over many years. I could face the government-sponsored execution or the greyest of golden years with a tranquil smile. I could immerse myself in the hope that I'd be welcomed through the pearly gates by a wizened old God; perhaps Baldr, Buddha, or Bacchus. Heaven is only what we wish for.

She would be there. The angel, the ruddy young cherub from the evidence photos. Even if she wasn't baptized. She'd be as I'd never seen her: whole, smiling. In jubilant tears I can't now imagine, I would walk past God to her and become her guardian until her parents followed their faith there, too.

But the truth is…just like me…they died when she did. From the day that angel's body was found so demonized on Earth, there never was a Heaven again.

12

Bloody Bloody

"**I**'m all bloody bloody!"

"That's just the kind of thing I'd expected from you!"

"Well, lassie, I'm positively drenched!"

"I'm covered too, and you don't see me bitching about it. You can wash your skort when we're done."

"Don't pretend ye don't know what a kilt is?"

"Sure, it's a lovely summer fashion, but a bit less useful for night hikes in the woods, don'tcha think? Grab those shovels! Whiny clod."

"What's that?"

"I said, grab the shovels!"

"No, after that, the muttery bit at the end."

"Hmm?"

"Do ye want the big shovel or the little one?"

"What do you think, you oaf? You're twice as tall as me and four times the weight!"

"Right, then. Well, let's break ground. Shallow graves don't be diggin' themselves!"

"You get started. I need to do something."

"What're ye doing? Are ye sneakin' off to hump them bodies while I'm not lookin', lassie? I'm no necrophile meself, but I don't judge! Aaahh-haah-ha-ha-ha-ahhh!"

"Why did I ask you to help me with this?"

"Ye couldn't find another psychopath on short notice. Aaahh-haah-ha-ha-ahh! What are ye doing over there? I'm diggin' all by me lonesome!"

"I'm cleaning up some of the evidence."

"Wha—have you got Windex over there?! What the hell do ye hope to accomplish with that?"

"Windex is good for cleaning...I always use it..."

"Aaahh-haah-ha-ha-ahh! Well, I'll be sure to bring ye along the next time I go a-window-washin!"

"Shut up! You have no idea. Just how many have you gotten away with?"

"Tonight's seventeen, eighteen, and nineteen."

"Well, I've killed...twenty-two people! So I know what I'm talking about!"

"All right, lassie, don't get your panties in a nit."

"Heeheeheeheeheehee...what? 'Panties in a nit?'"

"Granddad used to say that."

"Do you know what a nit is? It's like a louse... lice. 'Don't get yer panties in a headlouse!' Heeheeheehee!"

"You've got a laugh like a sputtering sparrow. It could wake a man after ten gallons o' scotch."

"I think I have a pretty laugh. And anyway, you sound like Santa wheezing up a lung."

"Aaahh-haah-ha-ha-ahh! Right ye are, lassie! If you're done playin' custodian over there, this hole's about dug."

"Yeah...should I, umm...get the gasoline and stuff?"

"Twenty-two, she says. Got a bit of tinder right at hand here...I'll set the fire. We'll put the bodies in first. Why don't you gather a bit o' wood?"

"Actually, I brought some! Back in a sec!"

"Ye brought your own wood? We're in the middle of the bloody State Park! Bit bloodier now, though, innit? Aaahh-haah-ha-ha-ha-ahh!"

"Here! Isn't this nicer?"

"Duraflames?! You're the blinkin' limit! Windex, fireplace logs...not sure if I'm at a crime scene or on Martha-bloody-Stewart!"

"Hey, I like how I do what I do. Just because it's the middle of the night and we're miles from civilization digging graves doesn't mean it can't be pleasant."

"I just can't believe ye brought Bed, Bath and Beyond out to the bloodsport! Are ye setting out candles now?!"

"They're lavender! Leave me alone, it'll help with the smell!"

"If you're looking to unwind, stay home and watch HGTV. We've got work to do."

"I can start the fire with these! They're useful!"

"You're daft."

"...said the psychopath."

"But I admit I'm daft."

"I think it's deep enough now. Shall we get them?"

"Aye. Grab the big one's legs."

"We made such a mess. At least he's the only teenager."

"Watch out, you're gonna-"

Schquuuopp

"Oh, no-no-no! All the organs! Oh, god, I'll get my dustpan and my grabber..."

"Dustpan? I've got a shovel right here! See? It's done, in the hole."

"God, I'm so sorry, I'm not myself tonight."

"It's nothing. I know how hard it is to tell, in the moment, how badly you're eviscerating 'em. Look, lassie! Swiss cheese!"

"Yeah, I had no idea how effective that egg beater would be."

"Aye, and the ice-cream scoop. Stroke o' genius!"

"The restaurant will never know we took this stuff; a little bleach is all we need. I think I have some in the car."

"That one I've got, lass. Standard bleach. Always bring a thermos full."

"You keep it in a thermos?"

"O'course. That way, it looks just like this one here, which is some tea I brought to wet my whistle. Here, wanna sip? Oh— Blechhhhk! This one's the bleach!"

"Oh, god, you drank bleach?!"

"Gotcha! Aaahh-haah-ha-ha-ha-ha-ha-ahh! Here, have a sip. It's naught but Twinings!"

"Oh, for fuck's sake. Let's get these other corpses in the ground."

"Right. Just the wee kiddies left. D'ye need my help with that one?"

"No, it's just about the size of my little boy."

"Oh, you've got kids?"

"Just my son, the light of my life! He's home with a sitter. What about you?"

"Twin girls, both seventeen. They've got me hair goin' grey with all the hormones."

"Wow, I hope my Emmitt stays my little baby forever. I'm not looking forward to him being a teenager. Children are so precious. Ready for the gasoline?"

"Whenever you are. Kids grow up. What can ye do?"

"Great, OK, a candle's going in!"

"Now, tha's lovely! Nothin' gets me up in tha mornin' like fresh wood smoke and corpses! And the hint of lavender is a nice touch!"

"Now, I guess we can just...sit and watch the fire?"

"Lassie?"

"I just...like watching fires with someone. My late husband used to take me camping a lot. I miss it."

"Shame, that. What happened to him?"

"I chopped him up with a salad knife after watching him kiss some woman on the cheek in a diner. Funny thing is, she turned out to be his eighty-five-year-old mother."

"What'd ye tell your son?"

"He was too young to really understand. I decided just to make burgers out of Rick's flesh. I figured that was a good way to let Emmitt say goodbye to his dad."

"Been quite the long time since I've eaten anyone. I'm usually in a hurry to cover things up."

"Well, maybe next time we'll bring a portable grill and—"

"Next time?"

"Well...it's been kinda fun, hasn't it?"

"We agreed it'd only be the one time, though,

lassie. I've had a good few laughs and all, but I'm a lone wolf."

"I know, I just thought—"

"Aye?"

"Well, to be honest, this is, please don't make fun of me, but this is my first time killing for fun and not just impulse."

"Twen'y-two times—"

"I know! I know! I felt like you'd judge me if I told you. I just wanted someone to come with me and make my first time feel less, I dunno, awkward."

"Well, to be honest, it was the opposite for me. Having someone here's been a wee bit awkward."

"I'm sorry. I guess I just wanted to feel cool, like you, like someone who knows what they're doing."

"Well, as I recall you did that by callin' me big and stupid and all that."

"I know...It's just kind of a reflex—when I'm trying to impress someone."

"Oh, ye were trying to impress me, were ye?"

"Well, you're a real serial killer! Me...I'm a kind of accidental one. My husband, my therapist, my brother and his fiancée...those were all spur-of-the-moment."

"Well, see, yer a killer born!"

"...and then there was every sitter I ever hired for my son...."

"Aaahh-haah-ha-ha-ha-ha-ahh!"

"This has been a blast. I know what we said, but I wouldn't mind doing this again sometime."

"Are ye asking me on a date?"

"Just killing, nothing serious."

"Let me give ye me business card so we can keep in touch."

"You're a lawyer? My mom always wanted me to marry a lawyer."

"Well, I hate to disappoint, but I married the love of me life twen'y years ago!"

"Oh, uh, I didn't mean—"

"Aaahh-haah-ha-ha-ahh! Goatcha again! She's been dead of leukemia for half a decade!"

"Look—the fire's starting to die. I can't really see anything but bone left."

"Aye, it's getting to be that time. Would ye like to cast the honorary first shovelful of dirt?"

"I guess. Where'd I leave that thing?"

"It's right here, where ye never touched it before!"

"Oh, cut it out. Let's get this over with. I hate manual labor."

"Just shovel it! Shovel the shite out of it!"

"Shovel that fuckin' dirt!"

"They'll never catch the likes of us!"

"Bury those bodies!"

"Bury 'em like a playha-haggis inna curt-o' Waughavanny!"

"What?"

"Sorry. That was me granddad again. You're a shovelin' maniac!"

"Heeheeheehee! That...was actually kinda fun!"

"You're even sweating! And I bet it took half the time it would've taken if ye'd dragged your feet and moaned about it til morning."

"So...I guess that's it?"

"Right. We've got quite the long drive now, though, followed by quite the long shower."

"Car's packed up. Let's be on our way. You know, it's really beautiful driving up here."

"Aye. I've been coming here since my third one. Got bodies all 'round these hills."

"I've lived in town all my life, never made the trek up here."

"That's what I count on!"

"I think I'll be coming back here a lot!!"

"Oh no! Now my best place'll be overrun with tourists!"

"No, I won't bring people up here! I mean, you know, to visit!"

"I suppose ye can have that hill over yonder."

"Nope, I'm going right back to yours; it's my favorite!"

"But, that one's mine! I got a special bond with them trees and squirrels and the wee baby deers!"

"Well, I just buried three people there, so it's half mine!"

"But I did half the killin', and more than half the buryin'."

"Call it a quarter then. But it's still part mine now!"

WEEEEoooEEEoooEEEoooo…

"Fuck me! It's the bleedin' paddy wagon! And we're still all bloody bloody!"

"Shitshitshit! OK, pull over really slow by that guardrail, nice and calm!"

"What are we going to do? We're covered in— Oh, hello, Officer!"

"License and registra—Step out of the vehicle! Ma'am do not move at all! Put your hands on the car! Why are you covered in blood!?"

"Well, ye see, Officer…I'm coming from me senior prom and all me classmates pulled a prank…"

"Put your hands behind your back, smart-ass!"

"Figured as much."

"Ma'am step out of the car right now!"

"Oh my god, please help me! He's crazy! He's crazy! He was gonna kill me!"

"Why are you covered in blood, too?"

"I'm the last one! He made me watch him kill the others! Ohhh, the things I've seen!"

"I need to ask you to calm down, ma'am, and understand that until I figure out what's going on here, I'll need to put handcuffs on you, too."

"OH, PLEASE NO! I've been tied up for the past two days!"

"Ma'am, stop whatever it is you're doing and step away from the vehicle!"

"Look, Officer! Here, in the trunk! Look what he used to kill them! Egg beaters and soup ladles and a tea strainer—OH GOD, THE TEA STRAINER!"

"Wha— Are those scented candles? Uh, ma'am, please step back. I need you to calm down—"

"Look, he's getting up!"

"Sir, sit down right now or I will shoot you!"

"Me nose itches! Come scratch it for me, laddybuck!"

"Sir, I'm going to place you in the back of my patrol car."

"Well you'll need to carry me like a wee baby, won't ye?"

"Come on...you can get up. There you go. OK, watch your head now—"

BDHUNCK

"'Bout time, lassie! I was wondering when ye were gonna do something useful."

"Oh, shut up, I had to get the trunk open to get at the shovel. He's just out cold, not dead."

"Well, don't just loll about! Get the keys to the cuffs!"

"Where are the keys?"

"Good god, lassie, did I dress him this morning 'fore he went off to school? How the devil should I know? Just get me outta here!"

"OK! OK! Stop yelling at me!"

"Oh for the love of Pete, they're in the blinkin' ignition!"

"Oh, yeah, that makes sense. Now let me just—"

"Ahhh, yes. I missed my wrists! Christ, he's coming to! Gimme that shovel!"

"Grab his gun!"

"That's no fun!"

DKSHKDD

"Wow! I'm impressed! Clean through the spine!"

"Now what in the seven hells are we gonna do with all this? I heard him calling more piggies."

"While you were freaking out in the car, I was planning. Beyond this guardrail is a nice deep ravine. Should provide an excellent dumping spot for the body, the car, everything."

"Fine, good enough. Let's just get it over with

and get home before they strap us inta the bleedin' electric chair. Ooof! Heavy bugger. Come on...grab his legs, we'll toss him in the trunk then boot the whole thing over."

"Ugh, this guy is so much heavier than those kids. Oh, shit! I kicked his head! Goddammit, it just rolled down into the ravine. Oh, well."

"Lassie, you're a right mess. Come on now, someone'll be by any second! I'll get the car pointed the right way. Always wanted to drive a cop car. Direct me."

"OK...just a little closer....little more..."

DUNNCKK

"Fucking hell, lassie, that's the edge! I thought ye liked me enough not to kill me, too!"

"Sorry! Sorry! It's dark!"

"Ye gave me a blinkin' heart attack!"

"I said I'm sorry!"

"Alright, It's in neutral, we've only got ta push it in."

"Alright."

"Come on, now, ye call that pushing? Me gran pushed harder when the tractor broke down."

"Fuck you! I'm trying as hard as I can!"

"Whew! Would ye look at that? The son of a bitch exploded! I thought that was just in movies!"

"We don't have time to ogle, I'm going to the

car."

"Suppose your right. Wonder if there'll be a forest fire on the telly tomorrow? Ye'd like to watch that, wouldn't ye?"

"Sure."

"What's wrong, I thought ye liked watchin' a fire?"

"I don't give a fuck about any fire!"

"This isn't about fire, then, is it?"

"No! It's about you yelling at me the whole time we were dealing with that cop!"

"Well, lassie, I've never been stopped before. And this was the first time I had a tag-a-long."

"Are you saying it's MY fault we got pulled over?!"

"I'm sayin' it never happens when I'm alone!"

"How dare you?! Like I wanted that to happen? I've got a little police radio in my purse? 'Come get us, cops, we're right here!'"

"I'm only saying you're a wee bit...clumsy."

"CLUMSY!?"

"You were clumsy with that lad's organs, you were clumsy kicking that cop's head...maybe ye made a mistake and that's why we got pulled over."

"Look. I'm sorry! I guess I get a little giddy around body parts. But that doesn't mean I caused—"

"We're close to town, now, and practically scot free. Let's just forget it."

". . . . ."

". . . . ."

"Close call, though, wasn't it, lassie?....So, what did ye think of your first time with the rope and the shovels and the whole serial-killer thing?.... Lassie?....Don't tell me yer still mad?....Lassie, look, I'm sorry if yelled at ye."

"It's fine."

"It's not fine. Ye wouldn't be giving me the cold shoulder if ye were fine."

"I can't believe you-hoo-hoo....!"

"Ah, now, don't cry, lassie. I'm sorry! I didn't mean for ye to feel bad."

"It's my first time! I was afraid I was gonna do something wrong and that's why I wanted you here in the first place...and now I'm just a complete fuck-up!"

"Oh no, no dearie, I didn't mean ye were a bad serial killer—"

"But you think I'm clumsy and stupid and you'll never want me around ever again!"

"Now, now, lassie dear. Dry your tears, please....I meant nothing of that sort. I was just scared we'd get pinched and only said all that tripe as I was upset. Me ol' thinker don't always choose the best o' words."

"You said it was all my fau-au-hault! But it's NOT!"

"Yer right as rain, lassie. I was likely just speedin', is all. It's probably me own fault at the heart o' the matter. I'm sorry, and I mean that."

"Well...at least we got away."

"Do I see a wee bit o' smile out the corner of me eye? Oh, aye, and it's getting bigger, there ye are! Here, let me find ye something that's not blood-stained for your tears."

"I have tissues in my purse. God, what a weird day it's been."

"To be sure. Can't believe only a few hours ago we were sneakin' those drugged RC Colas into that church barbecue. Well, we're back in town. You live down Oak Street, is that right?"

"Yeah, but actually, there's a gas station up here. We should pull in and clean the car."

"Right smart, lassie! Bit o' th' vacuum an' squeegee and we'll be on our way."

"Thank god the pumps are closed. Oh, wait! We can't get out! We're all bloody...bloody!"

"I hope that sounds less silly when I say it, aaahh-haah-ha-ha-ahh! Come on! We're just a couple of drunks out in the wee hours, playing with the hose!"

"Oh, god. Fine, you better be right. Is it coldaaaahh!!"

"Aye, it's brisk! Just turn around, so I can clean ye off."

"Ugh, now I feel like I'm at a wet t-shirt contest judged by Shrek."

"Now that was just mean! C'mon, dance around now, shake an' jiggle a wee bit!"

"Ugh! OK, turn it off! That's as good as I'm going to get. How are we gonna get all the blood out from the seats and stuff? I definitely didn't bring that enough Tide Colorsafe for everything."

"Lassie, watch this. Are you a busy maniac on the go? Tired of having to clean the blood out of your car seats? Presto!"

"Oh, it's a slip-cover! Nice American accent, by the way."

"I'll just toss this in the laundry later."

"You don't slay hard, you slay smart! OK, let's get home. I know a special little guy who's probably worried sick, if he's not asleep."

"Which way do I go?"

"Left, just head down this way. Hey...can I ask you something?"

"Fire away!"

"Does the...you know...screaming...ever get to

you? Does it bother you that...you know how bad it must hurt 'cause you've never heard a soul cry out like that?"

"Me? Not at all, I just pop on me headphones and listen to my favorite Miley Cyrus."

"No, but seriously. Doesn't it ever...mentally mess with you? Turn here, by the way."

"Lassie? Well, I don't know, that's a kind of a question, innit? Ye learn to enjoy it though, ye really do. It's like a developing a taste fer strange food. Make sense?"

"I guess. I mean, when we were killing those kids, and the youngest one was just like 'aaaaahh, please don't mister, please stop miss, help me Mommy!' It was just kinda hard. Especially as a mother myself."

"Oh dear, are ye having second thoughts? I hope you're not thinking about going to the police or anything. Will ye be alright?"

"I'm just really afraid that I might— GOTCHA! Heeheeheeheeheeheeheeheehee!"

"Oh, fer the love of— ye had me strung right along there, lassie!"

"Heeheeheehee! The look on your face! I want it in a photograph!"

"Aye, yes. It's a pity, this."

"What is?"

"We're here. Time to drop ye off, dontcha know. I had a lovely time, truly I did."

"That's it? I feel like a kid after a roller coaster ride. 'Let's go again'!"

"Well, ye've got me number and I've got yours, and—I hope to use it soon....Ye know, not to be creepy or anything. Just to kill people."

"Heeheehee!"

"Can I carry them melon ballers an' cheese graters to the door for ye?"

"Oh, that's sweet of you!"

"Well, lassie, I guess this'll be goodbye for now. ye look quite a sight in them bloodstained jeans, I—"

Mpwuaahh!

"Oh, ye make an old Scotsman all bloody ruddy! I was sorely tempted to kiss ye, little lassie, but you've beat me to it!"

"You know, the sitter's still here. I know we said we'd wait before doing any more killing together, but...would you umm...like to come inside?"

13

Not Dying

Today's a bad day.
There's no good anyone can say.
Nothing has been really going at all our way—

But I'm
OK.

We don't get to pray.
The sun lost its warmth from our ray.
We can only scowl beneath the moon-shine and
    bay—

But I'm
OK.

Folks yak, naught but "nay!"
Brutes, all, they surround us and bray.
They bleat loud in their judgment, lowing with
    dismay—

But I'm
OK.

We miss our old play.
You wait, I wait, far far away.
Softly beside yours my faint head I ache to lay—

But I'm
OK.

Our debt we must pay.
They'll leave us the bill on a tray.
We'll be stuck with the gross sum, not some trite
    copay—

But I'm
OK.

My head feels like hay.
My mouth and guts seem clogged with clay.
My heart pecks and flutters, bitter as a green
    jay—

But you're
OK.

Our future can fray.
Tomorrow is in disarray.
This bridge of our lives has an alarming new
    sway—

But you're
OK.

We don't know the way.
I can't think of what I should say.
Yet today has somehow still been another day—

Because we're
OK.

A NOTE TO READERS

◆ ◆ ◆

Thank you for letting me share my grief and my morbid sense of romanticism. If you loved what you read (or liked it, or even hated it for interesting reasons), please let me know by writing an honest review on Amazon. You'll not only be helping me honor my wife's memory and share my work, you'll be helping me get better. For more of my writing, and to connect with me personally, visit KevinChaba.com.

ACKNOWLEDGMENTS

I need to thank my wife for giving me both the inspiration to start writing and the impetus to publish. I'd also like to thank my editor Laura Ross for her invaluable guidance; my cover designer and my interior designer for making me look good; my parents for giving me the opportunity to write; Marcy for technical support and Mario for general support; Liz, Fuschia, Jasmine, Paul and Mary for their meaningful encouragement; Lifetime Care's grief resources and all the resilient people I've met through their support groups; Lesbian Vegan Space Porn for keeping me honest in my writing; my bookish and loquacious family; and the disturbed people the art comforts.

Amelia "Mia" Chaba

January 15th, 1988 – October 15th, 2015

She Will Be Loved